Vampire School
Casketball
Capers

For Theo and Tara
P.B.
For my family
C.H.

ISBN 978-0-545-30838-0

Based on an original idea by Chris Harrison.
Text copyright © 2010 by Peter Bently.
Illustrations copyright © 2010 by Chris Harrison.
All rights reserved. Published by Scholastic Inc., 557 Broadway, New York, NY 10012,
by arrangement with Boxer Books Limited. SCHOLASTIC and associated
logos are trademarks and/or registered trademarks of Scholastic Inc.

12 11 10 9 8 7 6 5 4 3 2 1   10 11 12 13 14 15/0

Printed in the U.S.A.   40

First Scholastic printing, October 2010

The illustrations were prepared using biro and watercolor paints.
The text is set in Blackmoor Plain and Adobe Caslon.

Vampire School

Casketball Capers

Written by Peter Bently

Illustrated by Chris Harrison

SCHOLASTIC INC.
New York Toronto London Auckland
Sydney Mexico City New Delhi Hong Kong

Contents

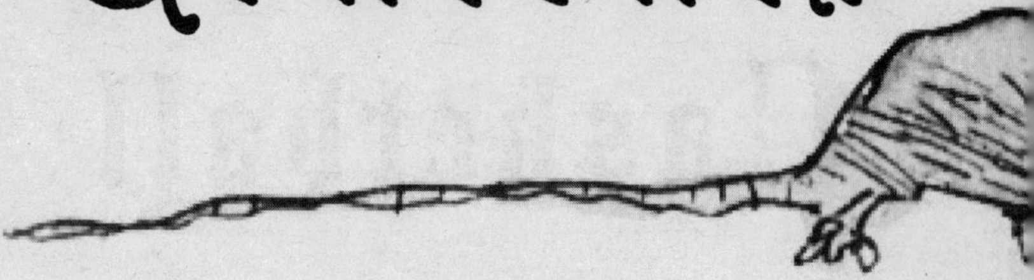

Chapter 1
School Time   8

Chapter 2
Bat Lessons   22

Chapter 3
Boris
the Bat   34

Chapter 4
Growler
the Fouler 50

Chapter 5
Mr. Tut
in a Tangle 64

Chapter 6
Boris to
the Rescue 76

Chapter 1
School Time

Lee Price was nine years old. He lived with his mom and dad in an ordinary house in an ordinary street and, like most nine-year-olds, he went to school every day.

Or rather, every night.

That's because St. Orlok's Elementary School was no ordinary school, and Lee was no ordinary boy.

St. Orlok's was a school for young vampires. Young vampires like Lee Price.

At St. Orlok's, Lee and his
friends learned to do all the
things that vampires do.

Like cloak-swishing ...

Scary staring ...

Tying a
bow tie ...

Losing your reflection ...

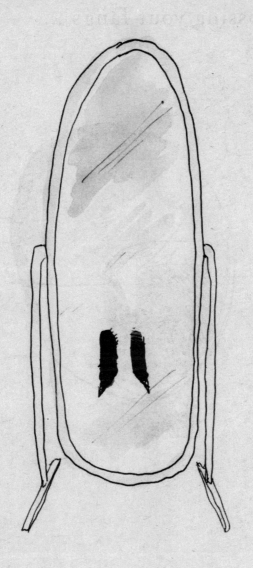

Flossing your fangs ...

And cooking without garlic.

Early one night, Lee's mom called up the stairs, just like she did every evening.

"Lee! Time to get up for school!"

Lee blinked sleepily in the bright moonlight.

"Aw," he groaned. "Just five more minutes!"

"No, dear. It's already ten past eight. If you don't get up now you'll be late."

Lee got dressed and went down to the kitchen for breakfast.

Dad was getting ready to go to work. He patted Lee on the head.

"See you later, Lee," he said. "Have a good night at school.

And good luck in the game. Don't let any of those werewolves near the casket!"

"Thanks, Dad, I won't," grinned Lee, gulping down a mouthful of blood orange juice.

Lee was on the St. Orlok's school casketball team. Casketball was the vampire version of basketball. Today they were playing in the Junior Inter-School Series against the werewolves of Chaney Street Elementary School.

With a little *POP!* Dad changed into a bat and fluttered out of the kitchen window.

Then Lee remembered.

"Hey, Mom! We're starting bat lessons today! We're learning how to turn into bats and how to fly. I can't wait!"

"Come on then," said Mom, looking at her watch. "Got your casketball uniform? Good. Now put your cloak on and run upstairs to comb your hair. And don't forget to brush your fangs."

Chapter 2
Bat Lessons

Mom left Lee at the gates of St. Orlok's. She gave him a peck on the cheek, said, "See you at half past three," then with a *POP!* she turned into a bat and flapped back home.

Lee ran to join Bella
Williams and Billy Pratt, his
best friends at school. They
were all in Miss Gargoyle's
class and very excited about
their first bat lesson.

"Being a bat will be great," said Lee. "We'll be able to fly to the tops of trees instead of climbing them."

"No way!" said Billy, who didn't like heights. "The best thing will be flying *really* fast."

"Did you know that there are over a thousand types of bats?" said Bella. "Mom bought me a book about it. I wonder what sort we'll turn into ..."

"Duh," said Lee. "*Vampire* bats, of course."

Lee, Billy, and Bella reached their classroom just as Miss Gargoyle was about to take attendance.

"Settle down now, children," said Miss Gargoyle. "Tonight I will show you one of the most important vampire skills—how to turn into a bat!"

The children all gathered around.

"First of all, you must think *really* hard about being a bat," said Miss Gargoyle. She closed her eyes.

"My arms are not arms but bat wings. My legs are little bat legs. My body is small and furry. My head is a bat's head with big bat ears. Got that?"

"Yes, Miss Gargoyle," chorused the class.

"Next, I say these words
to myself—

I'm a bat, a bat is me,
A bat is all I want to be."

With a soft *POP!* Miss
Gargoyle changed into a little
brown bat flapping in front of
the blackboard.

"See?" squeaked Miss

Gargoyle. "To change back, just say—

Pointy fangs

and swishing cape,
It's time to take on
vampire shape."

With another *POP!* Miss Gargoyle changed back into a vampire.

"Remember, don't *POP!* too loudly or Fangless folk might

hear," she said. "Right, now you all try."

Lee, Bella, and Billy soon found that changing into a bat wasn't as easy as it looked.

At first, Lee only managed to change his arms ...

and Bella changed everything except her head ...

Billy changed himself into a *cat* ...

and then a *rat*.

But finally there was a *POP!*
and suddenly Lee was flapping
around the room.

"I did it! I did it!"
he squeaked. "I'm a bat!"

Chapter 3
Boris the Bat

By lunchtime the classroom was full of little bats, giggling with glee.

"Well done, class!" said Miss Gargoyle. "After recess we'll practice hanging upside down. There'll be a little time before the werewolves arrive for the casketball game."

At recess Lee and his friends hurried outside. They couldn't wait to practice turning into bats.

It was a lot trickier without Miss Gargoyle there to help. First of all, Lee's left half became a bat but his right half stayed the same ...

Bella turned into a huge ball of bat fur ...

And Billy turned into a *bag*.

But at last they did it. With a *POP! POP! POP!* they were all fluttering around the playground.

"Come on," said Bella. "Let's
all play hide-and-seek! I'll
count to twenty." She shut her
eyes.

"One, two, three—"

Quick as a flash, Billy
darted out of sight. Lee looked
around for a hiding place. On
a window ledge? No, Bella
would spot him too easily.

"Four, five, six—"

Inside the school trash cans?
Poo! Too smelly!

"Seven, eight, nine—"

"Aha!" thought Lee. "Behind
the school gates!"

But Billy was already hiding
there.

"Buzz off, Lee!" he said.
"You'll give us both away!"

"Ten, eleven, twelve—"

"Yikes!" cried Lee. "This is harder than I thought!"

"Thirteen, fourteen, fifteen—"

DONG!
The school clock struck midnight.

"That's it!" Lee thought suddenly. "The clock tower!"

Where better for a bat to hide than in a belfry?

"Sixteen, seventeen, eighteen—"

Lee made it to the tower just as Bella cried, "Nineteen, twenty. Ready or not, here I come!"

Lee darted through a hole in the school clock—and bumped straight into another bat.

"Hey, watch where you're going!" said the bat.

"Sorry!" said Lee.

He didn't recognize the other bat so he said, "My

name's Lee. What's yours?"

"Boris," grunted the bat gruffly.

"Hi, Boris," smiled Lee. "I'm in Miss Gargoyle's class. Which class are you in?"

"Class?" snorted Boris. "Oh, I'm not one of you silly vampire kids. I'm a *real* bat."

"A real bat!" gasped Lee.

"Wow! Cool!"

"That's right," said Boris. "You vampires think you're so clever, turning into bats and all. But you can't do half the things a *proper* bat can do. Watch this!"

Boris folded his wings and dropped like a stone, all the way down to the bottom of the tower.

"Hey!" yelled Lee in terror. "Watch out!"

Boris was just about to hit
the ground when he opened
his wings and pulled up at
the last moment. He fluttered
back up to Lee.

"See?" said Boris. "Now off you go and play with those vampire friends of yours. Belfries are for *real* bats."

"But I'm supposed to be hiding," said Lee. "Can't I stay for a while? I'd *love* to learn some real bat tricks. They're so cool!"

Boris shrugged. "Well, all right. Just for a little while though. I don't want any of my friends to think I hang out with *vampires*."

Lee was delighted. With Boris to help he tried dive-bombing ...

looping the loop ...

and dodging things with his
eyes shut.

"Not bad," said Boris with
a grin. "Not bad at all. For a
vampire."

Just then the school clock

struck one.

"Yikes!" cried Lee.
"That was loud!" Then he
remembered. "One o'clock! I'll
be late for class! See you soon,
Boris. And thanks for the
tricks!"

Chapter 4
Growler the Fouler

Lee zoomed out of the belfry and back to his classroom. The others had already started to practice hanging upside down.

"Come along now, Lee

Price!" said Miss Gargoyle sternly. "You're late. Don't hang around. Or rather, *DO* hang around. Hurry up and find an empty place."

Billy and Bella had saved Lee a space on the curtains.

"Where were you hiding?" whispered Bella.

"Yeah, we couldn't find you anywhere," said Billy.

"I was in the clock tower," said Lee. "I met this *real* bat called Boris. He's so cool."

He was about to tell them more when they heard a *toot-toot* and saw a bus driving through the school gates.

"Look," said Bella. "The werewolves are here!"

"Aha!" said Miss Gargoyle,
fluttering over to the window.
"Lee, Billy, and Bella, you'd
better go and get ready for the
game. The rest of us will be
waiting to cheer you on!"

By the time the St. Orlok's team got changed, the Chaney Street werewolves were already out on the field warming up under the floodlights.

Lee jogged over to Ollie Talbot, his friend on the werewolf team.

"Hi, Ollie," he said. "Guess what? We had our first bat lessons today!"

"Cool!" said Ollie. "So this means you're even battier than usual."

"Ha-ha, very funny," groaned Lee. Ollie was always making terrible jokes.

Just then, a big werewolf pointed at them and sneered.

"Uh-oh, here comes Robbie Growler," sighed Ollie. "Just ignore him."

"What! Growler the Fouler?"
said Lee.

"That's him," said Ollie.
"The dirtiest player in Chaney
Street. He's our new Shooter."

There were two forwards, called Shooters, on each team, and they scored most of the points. The vampire Shooters were Bella, who was tall for her age, and an older girl named Naz Patel.

There were also three
Dodgers, whose main job was
to keep the ball away from
their own casket and pass it,
dribble it, roll it, or throw it
into the hands of the Shooters.
Billy, who was small and very
fast, was a fantastic Dodger.
The sixth player on each side

was the Ghoulkeeper, who defended the casket. That was Lee's job.

"Hey, Ollie," cried Growler. "Why are you talking to that sucker, huh? Get it? Sucker! Huh-huh-huh!" He loped up the field, snickering stupidly.

Lee was furious. He picked up a stick.

"Lee, no!" gasped Ollie.

"He'll make mincemeat out of you!"

Lee grinned.

"Don't worry, I'm not going to hit him. Just watch."

Growler turned around and snarled. Lee whistled as if he were calling a dog, then threw the stick toward him.

"Here boy!" he called. "Good boy! Fetch!"

The vampires all laughed, and so did Ollie and most of the other werewolves—when

Growler wasn't looking.

Bella and Billy were in stitches. Growler glared at Lee. "Come here, you little squirt," he growled. "I feel like a snack."

"Now, now!" said Mr. Tut, the mummy referee. "There'll be none of that, please! I want a good clean game!"

Chapter 5
Mr. Tut in a Tangle

The two casketball teams took up their positions. Mr. Tut blew his whistle and the game began.

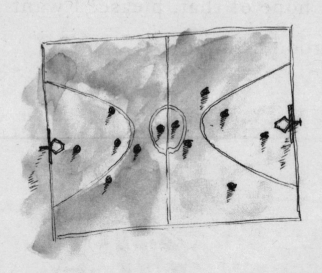

Billy got the ball and whizzed
past the three werewolf
Dodgers before bouncing it to
Naz Patel.

The vampires
cheered Naz on
as she charged
toward the
Chaney Street
casket—with Growler close
behind.

"Go on, Naz!" cried Lee.

Then he noticed that Growler
kept looking at Mr. Tut, who
was fiddling with a loose
bandage on his head.

"Growler's up to something,"
thought Lee.

He was right. Just then, the
loose bandage slipped over
the referee's eyes and Growler
grinned.

"Watch out, Naz!" cried
Bella, who was already up by
the Chaney Street casket.

It was too late. While
Mr. Tut was busy with his
bandages, Growler grabbed
the back of Naz's shirt and
punched the ball out of her
hands.

"That's a foul, ref!" cried the vampires.

But it was no good. Mr. Tut hadn't seen a thing.

"Thanks for the ball, sucker," cackled Growler, as Naz stumbled and fell to the ground. "Huh-huh-huh!"

Growler headed off toward
the vampire casket.

"Stop him, Billy!" cried Lee,
as Growler closed in on the St.
Orlok's Dodgers.

But the huge werewolf snarled
at Billy so fiercely that he
leaped out of his way in terror.

Now there was nothing between Growler and the casket except Lee. Growler made a move to the left, and Lee followed him. But then the werewolf quickly swung the other way, pounced high off the ground—and slammed the ball into the casket. The

werewolf supporters all cried
"Point!" and howled and
whooped in delight. Five
points to Chaney Street!

So it went on. Every time
Mr. Tut's loose bandage
slipped over his eyes, Growler
pushed, pulled, or tripped up
one of the vampire players and
kicked or punched the ball out
of their hands.

By halftime the vampires
still hadn't scored.

"It's no use," moaned Lee
as the teams went off for
the break. "We don't stand a
chance with Growler on their
side."

"I know," agreed Bella. "It's
not fair. He's such a cheat."

"Yeah, and the ref is as blind as a bat," said Billy.

"Blind as a bat," Lee said to himself, "I wonder ..."

With a *POP!* Lee suddenly turned into a bat.

"Back in five minutes!" he said, and flitted off.

"Hey, where's he going?" asked Bella.

"Dunno," said Billy. "Looks like he's heading for the clock tower ..."

Chapter 6
Boris to the Rescue

In the second half of the
game, St. Orlok's managed
to keep the werewolves from
scoring, but Growler made
sure that no one got anywhere
near the Chaney Street casket.

Even when he wasn't cheating,
he was so big and fierce that
most of the vampires were
terrified of him.

One minute from the end of the game, the score was still five-nothing, and it looked like the werewolves were going to win. Then Billy got the ball and skillfully bounced it to Bella.

"Go Bella!" cried Lee,
as Bella zipped past several
werewolves.

"Watch out for Growler!"
yelled Billy.

Sure enough, Mr. Tut
was soon fiddling with the
flapping bandages over his
eyes. Growler saw his chance

to cheat and thundered down
the court after Bella. But just
as he reached her, a small
black thing dived out of the
sky and grabbed hold of Mr.
Tut's loose bandage.

It was Boris the bat!

Boris lifted the bandage
just in time for Mr. Tut to see
Growler giving Bella a great
shove. With a SPLAT! she
landed on her bottom in the mud.

"Huh-huh-huh!" chuckled
Growler, running off with the
ball. "So long, sucker."

Mr. Tut was blowing his whistle.

"Foul! One penalty point to the vampires and a free throw at the casket!"

"Nice one, Boris!" grinned Lee.

"Don't mention it," said Boris.

Growler pointed angrily at
Boris. "Hey, ref!" he cried.
"One of them's changed into a bat!"

Turning into a bat was
against the rules. Any vampire
caught doing it would be
benched at once.

"Nonsense!" said Mr. Tut.

"Vampire bats have got big fangs. And besides, we'd have heard it go *POP*! This is a *real* bat. And very useful it is too. Play on!"

Suddenly the vampires had a chance. Growler glared at

Bella as she stepped up for the
free throw. She jogged into
the scoring zone, leaped—and
neatly dumped the ball into
the Chaney Street casket. Five
more points to the vampires!

Then, amid the cheers of the

vampires, Mr. Tut blew the final whistle.

The score was St. Orlok's 6, Chaney Street 5. St. Orlok's had won!

POP! POP! POP! POP!

Within seconds dozens of joyful vampires were turning into bats and flying over the field in glee.

"I'm glad we didn't win," said Ollie Talbot as the two teams left the field. "We didn't deserve to after all of Growler's cheating."

"Yeah," said Billy. "But where did that bat come from?"

Lee swished open his cape. Inside, hanging upside down, was Boris.

"Meet my new friend, Boris," said Lee.

"Hi, Boris," said Billy.

"Thanks for helping," said Bella.

"Well, I *do* hate cheating," said Boris. "That's something a real bat would *never* do."

"*Or* a vampire," said Lee. "It's just not fair."

Boris grinned. "I suppose you vampires are all right, really," he chuckled. "Even if you aren't *real* bats."

"Not real bats, huh?" laughed
Lee. "We'll soon see about
that."

Lee gave Billy and Bella
a funny look. They nodded.
Then, with a *POP! POP! POP!*
they all turned into bats.

"Right, Boris," cried Lee. "We'll race you to the clock tower. Last one there's a zombie!"

And the four bats zoomed off, laughing and giggling high above the roofs of St. Orlok's Elementary School.

The End

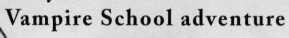